Tilly Turner
Champion Gurner

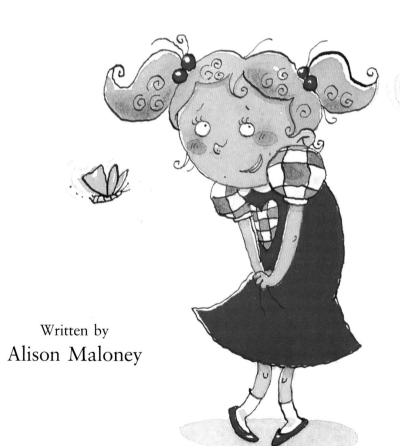

Illustrated by
Joëlle Dreidemy

Written by
Alison Maloney

meadowside
CHILDREN'S BOOKS

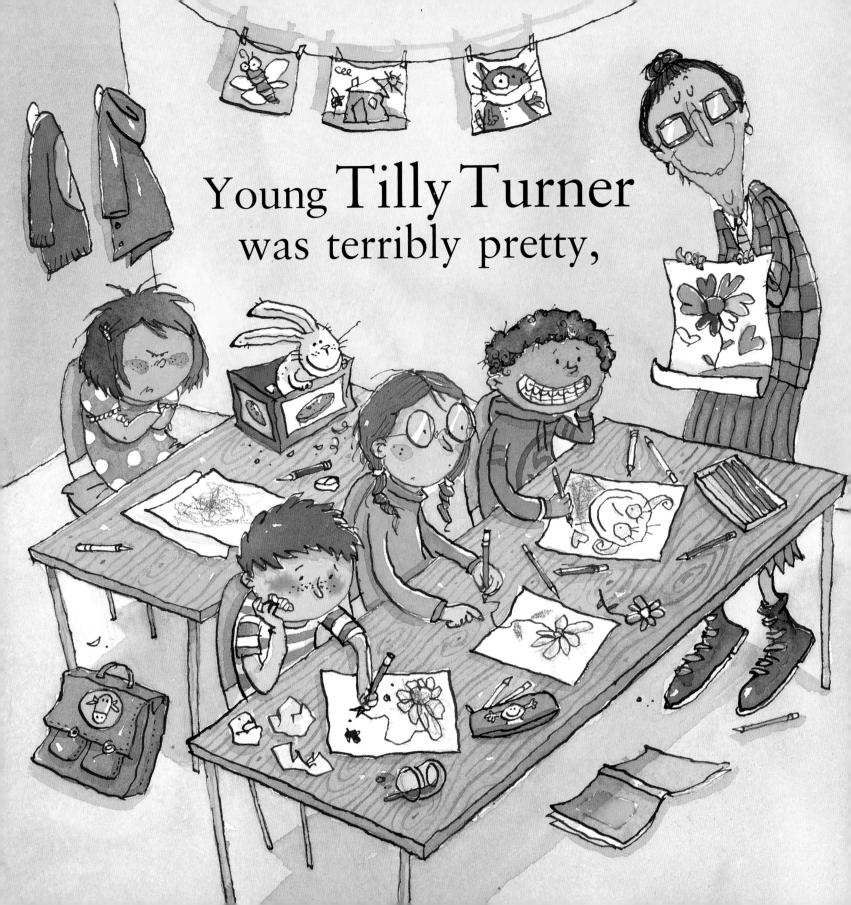

Young Tilly Turner
was terribly pretty,

Yet everyone saw her
and said,

"What a pity!"
She didn't have spots
or big metal braces...

But Tilly just loved to pull
horrible faces!

When she curled up her lip
and puffed out her cheeks,
The whole place erupted
in terrible shrieks!

When she stuck out her tongue
and rolled up one eye,
The children would flee
and the babies would cry.

"The wind will change soon,"
her mother would say,
"And one of your faces
will stay put that way."

Then one day
when Tilly was walking to school,
The sun disappeared
and the air turned quite cool.
Right out of nowhere
the slow-blowing breeze
Grew stronger and **stronger**
and whipped through the trees.

At the moment the wind changed
from **North East** to **West**,

The face she was pulling
was one of her best...

Her lips were all twisted,
her features agog.
Her eyes had POPPED out
like the ugliest frog.

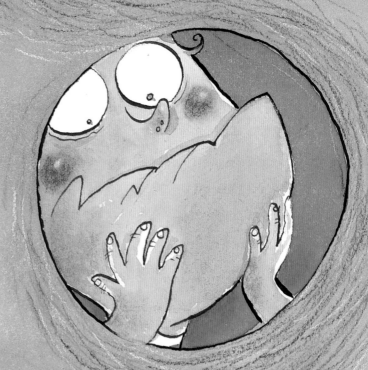

Her ears pointed up,
and her tongue pointed down.
Her eyebrows were creased
in a horrible frown.

Tilly continued her walk into school
(And we know that some children are terribly cruel).
As soon as they looked
at her hideous face,

They fell about laughing
all over the place.

The teachers appeared
and, with **horrified looks,**
Ordered the children
to pick up their books.

Then fierce Mrs Farthingale hollered **"Be quiet!"**

And told off poor Tilly for causing the riot.

Tilly ran out of school
in a terrible state,
And frightened the birds
who were perched on the gate.

The shopkeeper looked at
her face in dismay,
And passing dogs whimpered,
then scampered away.

The postman hid, the milkman cried,
Her next door neighbour ran inside.
Even her granny, her number one fan,
Took one look at Tilly and decided to scram.

Tilly ran off back home
where she hid and she cried.

But Mother said
"Tilly, I want you outside!"

So Tilly decided to wait on the path,
Ignoring the people who'd walk by and laugh.

But the wind started changing
from **North West** to **South**,
And Tilly felt something
relax in her mouth.

Then right up her nostrils
and all down her cheek,

A strange little tingle
made Tilly feel weak.

She waited for over
an hour to pass,
Then turned to a window
and looked in the glass.
And, to her relief,
she could see that her face
Had everything back
in its usual place.

She ran back inside
to escape from the rain,
And vowed that she'd
never pull faces again...

So that is the story
of young Tilly Turner...
No longer so proud
of her skills as a gurner.

For Georgia and Joe
A. M

For Yves Got
J. D

First published in 2005 by Meadowside Children's Books
185 Fleet Street, London, EC4A 2HS

Illustrations © Joëlle Dreidemy 2005

The right of Joëlle Dreidemy to be identified
as the illustrator of this work has been asserted
by her in accordance with the Copyright,
Designs and Patents Act, 1988

A CIP catalogue record for this book is available
from the British Library

Printed in U.A.E

10 9 8 7 6 5 4 3 2 1